To School

Written by Caleb Burroughs
Illustrated by Louise Gardner

Customer Service: 1-800-595-8484 or customer_service@pilbooks.com

www.pilbooks.com

Permission is never granted for commercial purposes.

p i kids is a registered trademark of Publications International, Ltd.

ISBN-13: 978-1-4127-9181-6
ISBN-10: 1-4127-9181-2

8 7 6 5 4 3 2 1

publications international, ltd.

Hi! My name is Ben. I'm going to school today. Would you like to come with me?

The big yellow school bus stopped at my house and picked me up. And now it has dropped me off at school.

"Good morning, children," says my teacher, Miss Harper. "Let's line up together. It's time to go inside."

In the classroom, we put our backpacks and lunch boxes away. Then we say the Pledge of Allegiance.

"It's circle time," says Miss Harper. My friends and I sit down on the round rug in the middle of the classroom.

Today we're playing Duck, Duck, Goose. Do you know how to play? It's my favorite game.

Next, it's art time.

There are many ways to make beautiful pictures.

My friend Maddie likes to use colored pencils. My friend Pedro likes to cut pictures out of paper. My friend Gina is busy finger-painting. How do you like my painting?

When we're finished, Miss Harper reminds us to clean up.

At noon, Miss Harper takes our class to the cafeteria. It's time for lunch!

Some of my friends bring their lunches in lunch boxes. Some kids buy lunch at school.

My mom packed my lunch in my lunch box. I have an apple and a yummy sandwich. Mmmm! She even wrote me a note that says, "I love you!"

After lunch, it's time to go outside for recess!

For recess, we go to the playground to play. Miss Harper watches us to make sure that everyone stays safe.

Some children are jumping rope. Others are playing catch. Can you see the kids swinging?

I like to play tag with my best friend, Jimmy.

When recess is over, it's time for us to settle down.

"Class, please sit down," says Miss Harper. "It's story time."

Everyone sits on the floor while the teacher reads us a story. Fairy tales are my favorite books, especially ones about brave knights, beautiful princesses, and scary dragons!

"The end," says Miss Harper when the story is over.

There are lots of other things to do at school.

There is a great big map on the wall. It shows where we live, and all sorts of other neat places around the world.

There is a computer in the classroom, too. We use it to learn—and to play games!

It's my job to feed the fish. Just a pinch of food is enough.

When the school day is over, the school bus brings me back home.

"I'm so proud of you," says my mom when I show her all that I did. I'm proud of me, too!